DOWN THE RABBIT HOLE

DOWN THE RABBIT HOLE

Juan Pablo Villalobos

Translated by Rosalind Harvey

Introduced by Adam Thirlwell

First published in English in 2011 by
And Other Stories
91 Tadros Court, High Wycombe, Bucks, HP13 7GF

www.andotherstories.org

Originally published as *Fiesta en la madriguera*
© Juan Pablo Villalobos, 2010
© Editorial Anagrama, S. A., 2010 Pedró de la Creu, 58 08034 Barcelona
English language translation copyright © Rosalind Harvey, 2011

ISBN 978-1-908276-00-1

A catalogue record for this book is available from the British Library.

This book is a work of fiction. Names, characters, businesses,
organisations, places and events are either the product of the author's
imagination or are used fictitiously. Any resemblance to actual
persons, living or dead, events or locales is entirely coincidental.

Supported by the National Lottery through Arts Council England.
This work has been published with a subsidy from the Directorate
General of Books, Archives and Libraries of the Spanish Ministry
of Culture.

LOTTERY FUNDED

For Mateo

CONTENTS

INTRODUCTION

If the international but anglophone reader tries to sketch a quick history of sudamericano fiction following the Boom of Márquez and Cortázar & Co, then two things become visible on this improvised map. On the one hand, it is now possible to see this Boom as having a past and a future. Its past was Borges, sure, but also Roberto Arlt and Felisberto Hernández and Macedonio Fernández; while the future is the fiction of Roberto Bolaño and Alan Pauls, Rodrigo Fresán and Ricardo Piglia. The past and future of this Boom represents a sequence of deft experiments. But there is something else to this sudamericano map: a sequence of market forces. As well as an array of experiments, there is also an array of pulp genres. And the most conspicuous of these is the one called narcoliteratura. Narcoliteratura is druglords and guns and girls. It is a corrupt and lurid politics.

And while it might at first look like this miniature novel by the Mexican novelist Juan Pablo Villalobos belongs to the second category of literary history – the pulp category of narcoliteratura, since its protagonists are a druglord and his psychopathic minions – it really belongs to the first: the history of experiments.

And so then: this is it.

This novel is narrated by a kid called Tochtli, the son of a druglord. And I suppose that the usual story, in this narco era, would be a story of drugs and police and gangs. But since this is a story narrated by a kid, it is therefore not at all a contribution to narcoliteratura. Instead, this novel tells the story of how Tochtli acquired a pair of Liberian pygmy hippopotamuses. Or at least: this is the story Tochtli thinks he is telling. But no story, in the end, is only the story it tells. Even Tochtli's story can't help leaking. Through his permutations of a limited set of perceptions and vocabularies, a devastated world emerges.

This novel is a miniature high-speed experiment with perspective. And so its essence is in its opening lines:

> Some people say I'm precocious. They say it mainly because they think I know difficult words for a little boy. Some of the difficult words I know are: sordid, disastrous, immaculate, pathetic and devastating. There aren't really that many people who say I'm precocious. The problem is I don't know that many people. I know maybe thirteen or fourteen people, and four of them say I'm precocious.'

Those five difficult words – sordid, disastrous, immaculate, pathetic, devastating – represent the elements of Tochtli's fugue. They represent its outline. Because he has crazes, this kid – like hats, and hippopotamuses, and words, and the Samurai. But these are the crazes he knows about. A person is not just a collection of conscious crazes; a person is overtaken by crazes of which they are unaware. So Tochtli's words, which seem to him to be a sign of his absolute freedom, are really a sign of his absolute entrapment.

Tochtli is a portrait of innocence; but he is also a portrait of absolute loneliness. This novel discovers innocence as loneliness. It discovers innocence as incomprehension.

There are precedents, I suppose, that the anglophone reader could consider, when considering this kind of machine: there is Lewis Carroll's *Alice in Wonderland*, with its reversals of proportion and perspective; and there is Henry James's *What Maisie Knew*, which recounts an adult story through the perspective of a child. But this novel represents something else.

In its investigation of innocence and knowledge, it is a deliberate, wild attack on the conventions of literature. Because literature, after all, prides itself on knowledge. It prides itself on depth. But knowledge is infinite, and so every depth is just another form of surface.

Tochtli's twin or shadow in this story isn't the demented figure of his father: no, his shadow is Mazatzin – his tutor. The life story of Mazatzin, says Tochtli, is 'really sordid and pathetic'. He was in TV advertising and he was rich: a man with millions of pesos. But since he always wanted to be a writer, Mazatzin

went to live very far away, in a cabin in the middle of
nowhere, on top of a mountain I think. He wanted to
sit down and think and write a book about life. He even
took a computer with him. That's not sordid, but it is
pathetic. The problem was that Mazatzin didn't feel
inspired and meanwhile his business partner, who was
also his best friend, scammed him out of his millions of
pesos. He wasn't a best friend at all but a traitor.

This short biography is a kind of anamorphic projection
thrown by Tochtli's own story. This is partly because of its
theme of treachery, but really because of its subject: that
dream of a book about life. For Tochtli is rightly if cutely scornful of Mazatzin's life story – a story which in his opinion only
proves that 'educated people know lots of things about books,
but nothing at all about life'. So when Tochtli strays once more
into literary criticism, he is again rightly if cutely scornful:

> Someone should invent a book that tells you what's hap-
> pening at this moment, as you read. It must be harder
> to write that sort of book than the futuristic ones that
> predict the future. That's why they don't exist. And
> that's why I have to go and investigate reality.

Yes, it is true, and it is also cute. Because Tochtli may be pre-
cise in his scorn, but he is no more intimate with life than
Mazatzin: he is no more able to investigate reality. The child
and the novelist are inversions of each other: they are both
bereft of the inside dope.

And yet . . . This is not the final lesson of this small novel. For Tochtli possesses something similar to knowledge, though not quite the same – his love of Liberian pygmy hippopotamuses. And this, in the end, is an advance. It is, possibly, a future. And the international, anglophone reader can measure this future by remembering a miniature moment in this miniature book about how miniature this thing called life can be. Early on, Tochtli presents a true and uncomprehending summary of killing – an unintended exercise in the deadpan: 'There are actually lots of ways of making corpses, but the most common ones are with orifices. Orifices are holes you make in people so their blood comes out.' The rest of this novel represents a confirmation of this sentence, but a confirmation that becomes a refutation: the deadpan is transformed into grief. Or, in other words, the matte linguistic surface of this novel – so limited, so inarticulate! – is converted into a form of truth.

Yes: something deadpan, innocent, damaged, matte, devastated: this, I think, is the great invention of Juan Pablo Villalobos in this tiny, comical space; and this is what might represent one future for an adequate fiction – a fiction adequate to what's happening. And not only in Sudamerica.

Adam Thirlwell
London, June 2011

DOWN THE RABBIT HOLE

ONE

Some people say I'm precocious. They say it mainly because they think I know difficult words for a little boy. Some of the difficult words I know are: sordid, disastrous, immaculate, pathetic and devastating. There aren't really that many people who say I'm precocious. The problem is I don't know that many people. I know maybe thirteen or fourteen people, and four of them say I'm precocious. They say I look older. Or the other way around: that I'm too little to know words like that. Or back-to-front and the other way around, sometimes people think I'm a dwarf. But I don't think I'm precocious. What happens is I have a trick, like magicians who pull rabbits out of hats, except I pull words out of the dictionary. Every night before I go to sleep I read the dictionary. My memory, which is really good, practically devastating, does the rest. Yolcaut doesn't think I'm precocious either. He says I'm a genius, he tells me:

'Tochtli, you're a genius, you little bastard.'

And he strokes my head with his fingers covered in gold and diamond rings.

Anyway, more people say I'm odd: seven. And just because I really like hats and always wear one. Wearing a hat is a good habit immaculate people have. In the sky there are pigeons doing their business. If you don't wear a hat you end up with a dirty head. Pigeons have no shame. They do their dirty business in front of everyone, while they're flying. They could easily do it hidden in the branches of a tree. Then we wouldn't have to spend the whole time looking at the sky and worrying about our heads. But hats, if they're good hats, can also be used to make you look distinguished. That is, hats are like the crowns of kings. If you're not a king you can wear a hat to be distinguished. And if you're not a king and you don't wear a hat you end up being a nobody.

I don't think I'm odd for wearing a hat. And oddness is related to ugliness, like Cinteotl says. What I definitely am is macho. For example: I don't cry all the time because I don't have a mum. If you don't have a mum you're supposed to cry a lot, gallons of tears, two or three gallons a day. But I don't cry, because people who cry are faggots. When I'm sad Yolcaut tells me not to cry, he says:

'Chin up, Tochtli, take it like a man.'

Yolcaut is my daddy, but he doesn't like it when I call him Daddy. He says we're the best and most macho gang for at least eight kilometres. Yolcaut is a realist and that's why he doesn't say we're the best gang in the universe or the best gang for 8,000 kilometres. Realists are people who think reality isn't how you think it is. Yolcaut told me that. Reality is like this and that's it. Tough luck. The realist's favourite saying is you have to be realistic.

I think we really are a very good gang. I have proof. Gangs are all about solidarity. So solidarity means that, because I like hats, Yolcaut buys me hats, lots of hats, so many that I have a collection of hats from all over the world and from all the different periods of the world. Although now more than new hats what I want is a Liberian pygmy hippopotamus. I've already written it down on the list of things I want and given it to Miztli. That's how we always do it, because I don't go out much, so Miztli buys me all the things I want on orders from Yolcaut. And since Miztli has a really bad memory I have to write lists for him. But you can't buy a Liberian pygmy hippopotamus that easily, in a pet shop. The biggest thing they sell in a pet shop is a dog. But who wants a dog? No one wants a dog. It's so hard to get a Liberian pygmy hippopotamus that it might be the only way to do it is by going to catch one in Liberia. That's why my tummy is hurting so much. Actually my tummy always hurts, but recently I've been getting cramps more often.

I think at the moment my life is a little bit sordid. Or pathetic.

I nearly always get on well with Mazatzin. He only annoys me when he's strict and makes me stick to our study plan rigidly. Mazatzin, by the way, doesn't call me Tochtli. He calls me Usagi, which is my name in Japanese, because he loves everything from the empire of Japan. What I really like about the empire of Japan are the samurai films. I've seen some of them so many times I know them off by heart. When I watch them I go on ahead and say the samurai's conversations out loud before they do. And I never get it wrong. That's because of my memory, which really is almost devastating. One of the films is called *Twilight of the Samurai* and it's about an old samurai who teaches the way of the samurai to a little boy. There's one bit where he makes the boy stay still and mute for days and days. He says to him: 'The guardian is stealthy and knows how to wait. Patience is his best weapon, like the crane who does not know despair. The weak are known by their movement. The strong by their stillness. Look at the devastating sword that knows not fear. Look at the wind. Look at your eyelashes. Close your eyes and look at your eyelashes.' It's not just this film I know off by heart, I know lots more, four.

One day, instead of teaching a lesson, Mazatzin told me his life story and it's really sordid and pathetic. What happened is that he used to do really good business in TV advertising. He earned millions of pesos by making up adverts for shampoo and fizzy drinks. But Mazatzin was always sad, because he'd actually studied to be a writer. This is where it gets sordid: someone earning millions of pesos being sad because they're not a writer. That's sordid. And so in the end, because he was so sad Mazatzin went to live very far away, in a cabin in the middle of nowhere, on top of a mountain I think. He wanted to sit down and think and write a book about life. He even took a computer with him. That's not sordid, but it is pathetic. The problem was that Mazatzin didn't feel inspired and meanwhile his business partner, who was also his best friend, scammed him out of his millions of pesos. He wasn't a best friend at all but a traitor.

That's when Mazatzin came to work for us, because Mazatzin is educated. Yolcaut says that educated people are the ones who think they're great because they know lots of things. They know things about science, like the fact that pigeons transmit disgusting diseases. They also know things about history, such as how the French love cutting the heads off kings. That's why educated people like being teachers. Sometimes the things they know are wrong, like if you want to write a book you have to go and live in a cabin in the middle of nowhere on top of a mountain. That's what Yolcaut says, that educated people know lots of things about books, but nothing at all about life. We live in the middle of nowhere too, but we don't do it for inspiration. We do it for protection.

Anyway, since I can't go to school, Mazatzin teaches me things from books. At the moment we're studying the conquest of Mexico. It's a fun topic, with war and blood and dead people. The story goes like this: on one side there were the kings and queens of the Spanish empire and on the other side there were the Indians who lived in Mexico. Then the kings and queens of Spain wanted to be the kings and queens of Mexico too. So they came and they started killing all the Indians, but only to scare them and make them accept their new kings. Well, the truth is they didn't even kill some of the Indians, they just burned their feet. This whole story makes Mazatzin furious, because he wears calico shirts and leather sandals as if he was an Indian. And he starts with one of his lectures. He says:

'They stole our money, Usagi, they plundered our country!'

It's almost as if the dead Indians were his cousins or his uncles. Pathetic. By the way, the Spanish don't like cutting the heads off kings. They still have living kings and queens with their heads stuck on their shoulders. Mazatzin showed me a photo in a magazine. That's really pathetic too.

One of the things I've learned from Yolcaut is that sometimes people don't turn into corpses with just one bullet. Sometimes they need three or even fourteen bullets. It all depends where you aim them. If you put two bullets in their brain they'll die for sure. But you can put up to 1,000 bullets in their hair and nothing will happen, although it must be fun to watch. I know all this from a game Yolcaut and I play. It's a question-and-answer game. One person says a number of bullets in a part of the body and the other one answers: alive, corpse, or too early to tell.

'One bullet in the heart.'

'Corpse.'

'Thirty bullets in the little toenail of the left foot.'

'Alive.'

'Three bullets in the pancreas.'

'Too early to tell.'

And we carry on like that. When we run out of body parts we look up new ones in a book that has pictures of all of them, even the prostate and the medulla oblongata. Speaking of the brain, it's important to take off your hat before you put bullets into somebody's brain, so it doesn't get stained. Blood is really hard to get out. This is what Itzpapalotl, the maid who does the cleaning in our palace, always says.

Yes, our palace: Yolcaut and I are the owners of a palace and we're not even kings. The thing is we have a lot of money. A huge amount. We have pesos, which is the money of Mexico. We also have dollars, which is the money of the United States. And we also have euros, which is the money of the countries and kingdoms of Europe. I think we have thousands of millions of all three kinds, although the 100,000-dollar bills are the ones we like the most. And as well as money we have all the jewels and the gems. And lots of safes with secret combinations. That's why I don't know very many people, maybe thirteen or fourteen. Because if I knew more people they'd steal our money or they'd scam us like they did to Mazatzin. Yolcaut says we have to protect ourselves. Gangs are about this, too.

The other day a man I didn't know came to our palace and Yolcaut wanted to know if I was macho or not. The man's face was covered in blood and, the truth is, I was a bit scared when I saw him. But I didn't say anything, because being macho means you're not scared and if you are scared you're a faggot. I stood there very solemnly while Miztli and Chichilkuali, who are the guards in our palace, gave him some devastating blows. The man turned out to be a faggot because he started to scream and shout, Don't kill me! Don't kill me! He even wet his pants. The good thing is that I did turn out to be macho and Yolcaut let me go before they turned the faggot into a corpse. They definitely killed him, because later I saw Itzpapalotl go past with her mop and bucket. I don't know how many bullets they put in him though. I'd say at least four in the heart. If I counted dead people I'd know more than thirteen or fourteen people. Seventeen or more. Twenty, easily. But dead people don't count, because the dead aren't people, they're corpses.

There are actually lots of ways of making corpses, but the most common ones are with orifices. Orifices are holes you make in people so their blood comes out. Bullets from pistols make orifices and knives can make orifices too. If your blood comes out there's a point when your heart or your liver stops working. Or your brain. And you die. Another way of making corpses is by cutting, which you can also do with knives or with machetes and guillotines. You can make little cuts or big ones. If they're big they separate the body parts and make corpses in little pieces. The most normal thing to do is to cut off the head, although, actually, you can cut anything. It's because of the neck. If we didn't have a neck it would be different. It might be normal to cut bodies in half down the middle so as to have two corpses. But we have a neck and this is a really big temptation. Especially for French people.

To be honest, sometimes our palace doesn't look like a palace. The problem is it's really big and there's no way of keeping it immaculate. For a long time Itzpapalotl has been wanting

Yolcaut to hire one of her nieces to help her with the cleaning. Itzpapalotl says she's trustworthy, but Yolcaut doesn't want any more people in our palace. Itzpapalotl grumbles because our palace has ten rooms: my bedroom, Yolcaut's bedroom, the hat room, the room Miztli and Chichilkuali use, Yolcaut's business room and five more empty rooms we don't use. And then as well as that there's the kitchen, the living room with the armchairs, the TV room, the cinema room, my games room, Yolcaut's games room, Yolcaut's office, the inside dining room, the dining room out on the terrace, the small dining room, five bathrooms we use, two we don't, the gym, the sauna and the swimming pool.

Miztli says Yolcaut is paranoid and that this is a problem. The problem has to do with keeping the palace clean and also with Miztli's time off. Because Miztli and Chichilkuali are in charge of protecting our palace with their rifles twenty-four hours a day. Twenty-four hours means that sometimes Miztli doesn't sleep and other times Chichilkuali doesn't sleep. Even though we have a really high wall to protect us. And even though on top of the wall there are bits of glass and barbed wire and an alarm with a laser beam that sometimes makes a noise when a bird flies close to it. And even though we live in the middle of nowhere.

Around our palace we have a gigantic garden. It's looked after by Azcatl, who is mute and spends the whole day surrounded by the noise of the machines he uses. The noise is deafening if you go really close. Azcatl has machines to cut the grass, machines to cut the weeds and machines to cut the trees and the bushes. But his main enemy is the weeds. The truth is Azcatl is losing the battle, because our garden is always full of weeds. By the way, Liberian pygmy hippopotamuses are silent machines that devour weeds. That's what's called being a herbivore, a plant-eater.

In the garden, opposite the dining room on the terrace, we also have cages with our animals, which are divided into two groups: the birds and the big cats. For birds we have eagles, falcons and a cage full of parakeets and brightly coloured parrots, macaws and that sort of thing. For cats we have a lion in one cage and two tigers in another. On the same side as the tigers there's a space where we're going to put the cage for our Liberian pygmy hippopotamus. Inside the cage there'll be a pond, but it won't be a deep pond, it'll just be for squelching around in the mud. Liberian pygmy hippopotamuses aren't like other hippopotamuses, which like to live submerged in the water. This is all going to be arranged by Itzcuauhtli, who looks after our animals: he gives them their food, cleans their cages and gives them medicine when they get ill. Itzcuauhtli could tell me lots of things about animals, like how to make them better and things like that. But he doesn't tell me anything: he's mute too.

I know a lot of mute people: three. Sometimes, when I tell them something, they look as if they want to talk and they open their mouths. But they stay quiet. Mutes are mysterious and enigmatic. The thing with silence is you can't give explanations. Mazatzin thinks the opposite: he says you can learn a lot by being silent. But those are ideas from the empire of Japan that he loves so much. I think the most enigmatic and mysterious thing in the world must be a Japanese mute.

Some days everything is disastrous. Like today, when I got the stabbing pain in my belly again. It's a sharp stab that feels like you're being electrocuted. Once I stuck a fork in an electric socket and electrocuted my hand a little bit. The stabbing is the same, but in my stomach.

To comfort me Yolcaut gave me a new hat for my collection: a three-cornered one. I have lots of three-cornered hats, eleven. Three-cornered hats are hats shaped like a triangle with a very small crown. I have three-cornered hats from France, from the kingdom of United and from the country of Austria. My favourite is a French one from a revolutionary army. At least that's what it said in the catalogue. I like French people because they take off the crown before they cut off their kings' heads. That way the crown doesn't get dented and you can keep it in a museum in Paris or sell it to someone with lots of money, like us. The new three-cornered hat is from the kingdom of Sweden and it has three little red balls, one on each point. I love three-cornered hats, because they're mad soldiers' hats. You put one on and you feel like running off all on your own to invade the nearest kingdom. But today I didn't feel like invading countries or starting wars. Today was a disastrous day.

In the afternoon Mazatzin didn't give me any homework and let me research a subject of my choice. It's something we do sometimes, mainly when I'm ill and find it hard to pay attention. I researched the country of Liberia. According to the encyclopaedia, Liberia was founded in the nineteenth century by people who used to work as slaves in the country of the United States. They were African American people. Their bosses set them free and they went to live in Africa. The problem was that there were already other people living there, the African people. And so the African American people formed the government of the country of Liberia and the African people didn't. That's why they spend their whole time fighting wars and killing each other. And now they're all pretty much dying of hunger.

It seems like the country of Liberia is a disastrous country. Mexico is a disastrous country, too. It's such a disastrous country that you can't get hold of a Liberian pygmy hippopotamus. Actually, that's what you call being a third-world country.

Politicians are people who make complicated deals. And they're not even precocious people, quite the opposite. That's what Yolcaut says, that to earn millions of pesos you don't need to repeat the word 'democracy' so many times. Today I met the fourteenth or fifteenth person I know and he was a politician called the Governor. He came to have dinner at our palace because Cinteotl makes a really tasty green pozole. Cinteotl is the cook at our palace and she knows how to make all the types of pozole that exist in the world, which is three: the green kind, the white kind and the red kind. I don't like pozole much, mainly because it's got cooked lettuce in it, which is ridiculous. Lettuce is for salads and sandwiches. Also you make pozole with pigs' heads: once I peeped into the pot and there were teeth and ears floating around in the broth. Sordid. The things I like are enchiladas, quesadillas and tacos *al pastor*. I like tacos *al pastor* without the pineapple, because pineapple on a taco is ridiculous too. I hardly put any chilli on my enchiladas, because otherwise my belly hurts a lot.

The Governor is a man who thinks he governs the people who live in a state. Yolcaut says the Governor doesn't govern anyone, not even his fucking mother. In any case the Governor is a nice man, although he has a tuft of white hair in the middle of his head that he doesn't shave off. I had fun listening to Yolcaut and the Governor talking. But the Governor didn't. His face was all red, as if it was going to explode, because I was eating some quesadillas while they had green pozole and talked about their cocaine business. Yolcaut told him to calm down, that I was old enough, that we were a gang and in gangs you don't hide the truth. Then the Governor asked me how old I was and when I told him he decided I was still too young to know about that sort of thing. That was when Yolcaut lost his temper and threw a whole load of dollar bills from a bag into the Governor's face. There were lots of them, thousands. And he started to shout at him:

'Shut the fuck up, Governor, what the fuck do you know? Go on, you bastard, take your money, you asshole.'

Then he told me that's what our business was for, for bankrolling assholes. The Governor's face went even more red, as if he really was going to explode, but he started to laugh. Yolcaut said if he was so worried about me then he should get me a hippopotamus. The Governor made a face like he didn't understand a thing, so I explained that what I wanted was a Liberian pygmy hippopotamus, which is very hard to get hold of without going to the country of Liberia. His face stopped looking like it was going to explode. He asked us: 'And why don't you go to Liberia?' Yolcaut just replied:

'Don't be an asshole, Governor.'

Then the Governor said:

'Let's see, we might be able to sort something out.' And Yolcaut stroked my head with his fingers covered in gold rings and diamonds.

'You see, Tochtli: Yolcaut always finds a way.'

The truth is, sometimes Mexico is a wonderful country where you can do really good deals. That is, sometimes Mexico is a disastrous country, but sometimes it's a wonderful country, too.

One song I love is 'The King'. It was even the first song I learned by heart. And back then I was really little and my memory wasn't even devastating yet. The truth is I didn't know it that well, but I used to make up the bits I couldn't remember. The thing is it's really easy to rhyme in this song. For instance: king and sing rhyme. If you swap one word with another, no one will notice. The bit I like in 'The King' is the part where it says I don't have a throne or a queen for my wife, or someone who pays for the things in my life, but I'm still the king. That's where it explains the things you need in order to be king: a throne, a queen and someone to support you. Although when you sing the song you don't have any of this, not even money, and you're still king, because your word is law. That's because the song's really about being macho. Sometimes macho men aren't afraid and that's why they're macho. But also sometimes macho men don't have anything and they're still kings, because they're macho.

The best thing about being a king is that you don't have to work. All you have to do is put on your crown and that's it, the people in your kingdom give you money, millions and millions. I've got a crown, although I'm not allowed to wear it every day. Yolcaut's only let me put it on four times. We keep it in a safe with all our treasure. The crown isn't made of gold, because it belonged to a king from Africa and in Africa everyone is poor, even the kings. The country of Liberia is in Africa. The good thing is that Mexico isn't in Africa. It would be disastrous if Mexico was in Africa. The crown is made of metal and diamonds. It cost us a lot of money because to be a king in Africa you have to kill lots of people. It's like a competition: the one who wears the crown is the one who's made the most corpses. Mazatzin says it's the same in Europe. This subject also makes him furious and inspires him to give lectures. Mazatzin wasn't inspired to write a book at the top of his mountain, but he was inspired to give lectures, which he does all the time. He says:

'Europe is built on a mountain of corpses, Usagi, rivers of blood flow through Europe.'

When we talk about these things you can see Mazatzin hates the Spanish and sometimes even the French. All

Europeans. Pathetic. I think the French are good people because they invented the guillotine. And the Spanish are good
customers of Yolcaut's business. But the Gringos are better
customers. The Mexicans are not good customers for Yolcaut,
because Yolcaut refuses to do business with them. One of
the corpses I met was a security guard who used to do what
Chichilkuali does, but he decided to start doing business in
Mexico. Yolcaut doesn't want to poison the Mexicans. Mazatzin says that's what's called being a nationalist.

The mutest person I know is Quecholli. Miztli brings her to
our palace two or three times a week. Quecholli has really
long legs, according to Cinteotl this long: one and a half
metres. Miztli says something else, something enigmatic:
'Thirty-six, twenty-four, thirty-six.'
It's a secret, he says it to me when no one's listening.
Everything about Quecholli is a secret. She walks around the
palace without looking at anyone, without making a sound,
always clinging to Yolcaut. Sometimes they disappear and
then reappear, really mysterious. They spend hours like that,
the whole day, until Quecholli leaves. Then Miztli brings her
back again and it's back to the secrets and disappearing.
The most enigmatic time is when we all sit down together to eat on the terrace: Yolcaut, Quecholli, Mazatzin and me.
The first time, Mazatzin asked Quecholli if she was from León
or Guadalajara or wherever. Quecholli didn't say a thing. She
looked at Mazatzin for a second and then Yolcaut shouted that
she was from the motherfucking house of the rising sun.

It might seem like Quecholli is blind too, because you almost never know which direction she's looking in. But she's not blind: I've seen her looking at my hats. Another strange thing is that she only eats salad. Her favourite is a salad with lettuce, tomato, broccoli, onion and avocado. Then she adds lime juice and salt with those long thin fingers she has. Covered in rings. But Quecholli's rings are delicate and really tiny, not like Yolcaut's, which are thick and have gigantic diamonds on them. She's not a millionaire like us.

Over dinner Yolcaut and Mazatzin talk about politicians. It's a funny conversation because Yolcaut laughs a lot and tells Mazatzin he's so fucking gullible. Mazatzin doesn't laugh as much, because he thinks we should have a government of left-wing politicians. He says: 'If the left was in power this wouldn't happen.' Yolcaut laughs some more. Some days Mazatzin says the names of politicians to Yolcaut and, depending on the name, Yolcaut replies:

'Mm-hmm.'

Or:

'Uh-uh.'

Sometimes Mazatzin looks surprised and laughs and says I knew it, I knew it. Other times he shouts Liar, liar, and Yolcaut tells him he's so fucking gullible.

While Quecholli eats her salad the rest of us eat whatever delicacy Cinteotl has made. Mazatzin loves her cooking. When he's finished he shouts for Cinteotl and tells her that was the best *mole* of his life, if we ate *mole*, or the best *tampiqueña*, or whatever it was. Pathetic. Yolcaut thinks being hungry is in Mazatzin's genes. Quecholli, since she's mute, says nothing. Mazatzin says she's a vegetarian. I say she's like the Liberian pygmy hippopotamuses, a herbivore. But Liberian pygmy hippopotamuses don't like lettuce salads, they like alfalfa salads. If Quecholli wasn't mute I'd ask her opinion on the hot lettuce in the pozole.

This is what was on the news today on the TV: the tigers in the zoo in Guadalajara ate a woman all up, apart from her left leg. Maybe her left leg wasn't a very juicy bit. Or maybe the tigers were already full up. I've never been to the zoo in Guadalajara. Once I asked Yolcaut to take me, but instead of taking me he brought more animals to the palace. That was when he bought me the lion. And he said something to me about a man who couldn't go to a mountain and so the mountain came to him.

The eaten woman was the head zookeeper and she had two children, a husband and international prestige. That's a pretty word, prestige. They said it might have been suicide or murder, because she never used to go into the tigers' cage. We don't use our tigers for suicides or for murders. Miztli and Chichilkuali do the murders with orifices made from bullets. I don't know how we do the suicides, but we don't do them with tigers. We use the tigers for eating the corpses. And we use our lion for that too. But we mainly use them for looking at, because they're strong and really well-proportioned animals and they're nice to look at. It must be because they're so well fed. I'm not supposed to know these things, because they're secrets Miztli and Chichilkuali do at night. But in that way I do think I'm precocious, in discovering secrets.

At the end of the report the man on the news looked very sad and said he hoped the head zookeeper would rest in peace. How stupid. She was already chewed up inside the tigers' tummies. And she's only going to stay there while the tigers digest her, because she'll end up being turned into tiger poo. Rest in peace, like hell. At the most her left leg will rest in peace.

Yolcaut watched the news with me and when it was over he said some enigmatic things to me. First he said:

'Ah, they suicided her.'

And then, when he'd stopped laughing:

'Think the worst and you'll be right.'

Sometimes Yolcaut speaks in enigmatic and mysterious sentences. When he does that it's pointless to ask him what he means, because he never tells me. He wants me to solve the enigma.

Before I went to sleep I looked up the word prestige in the dictionary. I learned that prestige is about people having a good idea about you, and thinking you're the best. In that case you have prestige. Pathetic.

Today I'm devastatingly desperately bored. I'm bored because I don't leave the palace and because every day is the same.

I get up at eight o'clock, I wash and I have breakfast.
From nine to one I have lessons with Mazatzin.

I play on the Playstation from one to two.

Between two and three we have lunch.

From three to five I do my homework and research my own subjects.

From five to eight I do whatever I can think of.

At eight o'clock we have dinner.

From nine to ten I watch TV with Yolcaut and then after ten o'clock I go to my room to read the dictionary and go to sleep.

The next day is the same. Saturdays and Sundays are the worst, because I spend the whole day waiting to see what I can think of to do: going to see our animals, watching films, talking about secret things with Miztli, playing on the Playstation, cleaning my hats, watching TV, making lists of the things I want so Miztli can buy them for me . . . Sometimes it's fun, but also sometimes it's disastrous. Because of Yolcaut's paranoia I haven't been out of the palace for quite a few days, eleven.

It all began when they showed soldiers looking for drugs on the news. Chichilkuali said to Yolcaut:

'Problems, boss.'

Yolcaut told him not to be an asshole. The next day on the TV they said that some men who were in prison in Mexico had been sent to live in a prison in the country of the United States as a surprise. Yolcaut started to pay really close attention to the news and he even asked me to be quiet. On the TV they were showing a list with the names of the men who now lived in the prison in the country of the United States.

When the report was over Yolcaut said one of his enigmatic and mysterious phrases. He said:

'The shit's really hit the fan now.'

It was a really enigmatic phrase, because even Chichilkuali went quiet with a face like he wanted to decipher the mystery.

Since then there've been corpses on the TV every day. They've shown: the corpse in the zoo, corpses of policemen, corpses of drug traffickers, corpses from the army, corpses of politicians and corpses of fucking innocent people. The Governor and the president went on TV to tell all us Mexicans not to worry, to stay calm.

Yolcaut hasn't been out of the palace either. He spends all his time talking on the phone giving orders. Miztli and Chichilkuali have been out of the palace. Miztli says it's fucking chaos outside. Chichilkuali says there are fuckloads of problems. Yolcaut wants us to go on a trip to a faraway place for a while, for protection. He asked me where I wanted to go and promised me we'd go wherever I wanted. Mazatzin advised me to ask to go to the empire of Japan. If we went there I could meet a Japanese mute. But I want to go to the country of Liberia to go on safaris and catch a Liberian pygmy hippopotamus.

Mazatzin has been reading me bits from an old futuristic book. It's a book a man wrote many years ago imagining the time we live in now. And so it's really funny because the author guessed lots of things that happen today, like hair transplants and cloning. But Mazatzin thinks the things the author didn't guess are funnier, like the thing about hats. In the book everyone wears hats. Mazatzin thinks it's really funny how the writer was able to imagine difficult things and couldn't imagine that people would stop wearing hats. And he said it's as if we were all walking around today wearing sombreros like charro horsemen. Poor Mazatzin. Educated people really do know a lot of things from books, but they know nothing about life. This wasn't the writer's mistake. It was humanity's mistake.

I've got lots of charro sombreros, six. One of them is a famous sombrero because a charro wore it in a really old film. Yolcaut bought me the sombrero for my birthday last year and then we watched the film to look for the sombrero. The film's about two charros fighting over a woman. It's a really ridiculous film. Instead of fighting with bullets the two horsemen fight with songs. And they're not even macho songs, like 'The King'. That's what I don't understand: if they're charros and macho why do they sing love songs as if they were faggots? Maybe that's why no one wants to wear a hat anymore, because people used to do ridiculous things like wearing charro sombreros and being faggots. That's when hats stopped being prestigious. At the end of the film the two charros both end up happy, each with a different woman. They even make friends and live happily ever after: totally ridiculous.

The problem with this film is that it's Yolcaut's favourite and he makes me watch it with him whenever he feels like it.

We've seen it loads of times, easily twenty. I've already learned it by heart without meaning to. The worst part is when one of the charros goes up to the woman's window and says things about love to her. He says: 'Your eyes are like starlight, two bright orbs that light up my darkness. I know I don't deserve you, but without you life is a torment, an eternal dying.' Pathetic. The other charro sombrero I've got was a present from Miztli, also for my birthday last year. My birthday last year was disastrous. I got so many charro sombreros it was as if I was a nationalist. This other sombrero was made in Miztli's village, which according to him is a charro village. But it's a lie. In charro villages there have to be at least 1,000 horsemen.

One day, a long time ago, Miztli took me to his village and we didn't see one horse. And there were zero people wearing charro sombreros, zero. There were lots of shops selling charro sombreros and things for horses. One of the shops was called El Charro, another was called Charro World, another Charro Gear and another one Charrito's. But there weren't any charros, there were people taking photos and buying keyrings and postcards. The only charro I saw was a statue at the entrance to the village. He was a suspect charro, because it looked like he was dancing ballet like a faggot. And he didn't even have a hat. Miztli said someone had stolen it, that one morning the charro woke up without his hat. The thief must have been one of those people who think charros shouldn't be faggots.

In any case Miztli was really happy to show me his so-called charro village. Pathetic. The truth is, there were more churches than anything else in the village. There were so many churches that instead of a charro village it was a priest village. Miztli thought this was really funny. He said yes, it was a priest village, but they were macho priests. And then he pointed out a little boy who was walking down the street and said:

'Look, look, that's the bishop's son.'

The problem with charro sombreros is they're only for charros. The thing is that the brim is very wide, they might even have the widest brim of all the hats in the world. I think if there was a hat with a wider brim it wouldn't be a hat any more. It would be a parasol.

If you're not a charro and you put on a charro sombrero you might get dizzy and fall over. Then, with your charro sombrero on, it's really difficult to get up off the floor. Other people put on charro sombreros and they go mad. But not mad for invading countries, like with the three-cornered hats. Really just for shooting bullets into the sky and shouting nationalist slogans.

But the charros don't fall over or go mad. They stay in the shadow of their sombreros, very mysterious and enigmatic.

Who knows what the charros are hiding from.

Who know what they're plotting.

Today there was an enigmatic corpse on the TV: they cut off his head and he wasn't even a king. It didn't look like it was the work of the French either, who like cutting off heads so much. The French put the heads in a basket after cutting them off. I saw it in a film. They put a basket just under the king's head in the guillotine. Then the French let the blade fall and the king's head is cut off and lands in the basket. That's why I like the French so much, they're so refined. As well as taking off the king's crown so it doesn't get dented, they take care that his head doesn't roll away from them. Then the French give his head to some lady to make her cry. A queen or a princess or something like that. Pathetic.

We Mexicans don't use baskets when we cut off heads. We hand over the severed heads in a crate of vintage brandy. Apparently this is very important, because the man on the news repeated over and over that the head had been delivered in a crate of vintage brandy. The head was from the corpse of a policeman, the chief of all the policemen or something like that. Nobody knows where the other parts of the corpse went.

On the TV they showed a photo of the head and the truth is he had a really bad hairstyle. He had long hair with a few strands dyed blond, pathetic. Hats are good for that too, for hiding your hair. Not just when it's a bad hairstyle, because it's best to hide your hair all the time, even with supposedly nice hairstyles. Hair is a dead part of the body. For example: when you get your hair cut it doesn't hurt. And if it doesn't hurt it's because it's dead. It does hurt when someone pulls it, but it's not the hair that hurts, it's your scalp. I researched it in my free time with Mazatzin. Hair is like a corpse you wear on your head while you're alive. And it's a devastating corpse that grows and grows without stopping, which is very sordid. Maybe when you turn into a corpse your hair isn't sordid any more, but before it is. That's the best thing about Liberian pygmy hippopotamuses: they're bald.

I don't have hair for that reason. Yolcaut shaves it with a razor as soon as it starts to grow. The razor is the same as the machine Azcatl uses to cut the grass, but small. And hair is like the weeds you have to fight. Sometimes Yolcaut gets annoyed because I ask him to shave my head really often. Bald people are definitely very lucky.

These are the things you can hide under a detective hat: your hair, a baby rabbit, a tiny little gun with minuscule bullets, a carrot for the baby rabbit. Detective hats aren't very good hiding places. If you need to put a rifle with gigantic bullets in there it won't fit. The best hats for hiding things in are top hats, like the ones magicians wear. But detective hats are good for solving enigmas and mysteries. I've got lots of detective hats, three. I put them on whenever I find out mysterious things are going on in the palace. And I start to investigate, stealthily. It's not like the research I do with Mazatzin, because I do that with books. Books don't have anything in them about the present, only the past and the future. This is one of the biggest defects of books. Someone should invent a book that tells you what's happening at this moment, as you read. It must be harder to write that sort of book than the futuristic ones that predict the future. That's why they don't exist. And that's why I have to go and investigate reality.

Today Miztli and Chichilkuali did mysterious things, like filling a truck with crates they took out of one of the empty rooms we don't use. When they left I put on a detective hat and discovered one of Yolcaut's enigmas. The empty rooms we don't use are always locked, but today one was left open. And it turns out we don't have five empty rooms we don't use, only four, or none: one of the empty rooms we don't use is really the gun and rifle room.

The guns are hidden in drawers and the rifles are hidden inside a cupboard. I didn't have time to count them, because I didn't want Yolcaut to find me, but we must have at least about 1,000 guns and about 500 rifles. We've got all different sizes, we even have a rifle with gigantic bullets. That's when I realised Yolcaut and I are playing the bullet game wrong: with a bullet from that rifle you'd definitely turn into a corpse, it wouldn't matter where it got you, apart from the hair, which is already dead. We should play the bullet game saying the number of bullets, the part of the body and the size of the bullet. A little orifice, where it would take five days for all the blood to come out, isn't the same as an enormous orifice, where it'd take five seconds. I also found a tiny little pistol with some bullets so minuscule that even if it shot you seventy times in the heart you still wouldn't be a corpse.

If I'd known what I was going to find in the gun and rifle room I wouldn't have put on a detective hat. I would have put on the highest top hat from my hat collection, one you could fit about six or seven rabbits in. I would have liked to hide the rifle with gigantic bullets under my hat, but all I could take was the tiny little pistol with the minuscule bullets. Disastrous. But the most disastrous thing of all was finding out

Yolcaut is telling me lies, like saying we have empty rooms when they're really rooms with guns and rifles in them. Gangs are not about lies. Gangs are about solidarity, protection and not hiding the truth from each other. At least that's what Yolcaut says, but he's a liar. I don't think I'm even going to get a Liberian pygmy hippopotamus. Or go to the country of Liberia. They must be more of Yolcaut's lies.

When I can't bear the pain in my tummy, like today, Cinteotl makes me a cup of chamomile tea. Sometimes I get such bad pains I even start crying. Normally they're like cramps, although the worst ones feel like a hole that keeps growing and growing and it's as if my tummy's going to explode. I always cry when I get these pains, but I'm not a faggot. Being ill is different to being a faggot. If you're ill it's all right to cry, Yolcaut told me.

Cinteotl has a drawer full of herbs for curing illnesses. She's got chamomile for the stomach, linden flowers for nerves, orange leaves for dieting, passionflower for nerves, orange blossom for digestion, valerian for nerves and a load of other herbs, lots of them for nerves. Yolcaut doesn't like tea, he says it's a coward's drink.

Yolcaut used to prefer Miztli to get the doctor when my tummy hurt a lot. The doctor was quite an old man and when Yolcaut wasn't looking he used to slip me tamarind sweets. And I'm not even allowed to eat tamarind. Or chilli. According to the doctor, there was something wrong with my psychology, not my tummy.

The best thing about the doctor was he told some really funny stories about aliens. Once aliens came to León in their spaceship. They landed in a field of corn to collect plants and animals. In the place where the spaceship landed they left a burnt patch where no plants have ever grown again, not even grass. And this was many years ago, more than four, I think. Another time the aliens came to abduct a little girl. And another time they were hovering above Aguascalientes for an hour.

The doctor doesn't come any more because Yolcaut got annoyed with him. Once, according to Miztli, the doctor told Yolcaut it wasn't really my stomach making me ill, but that the pains came from not having a mummy, and what I needed was a psychology doctor. Supposedly this is what's called a psychosomatic illness, which means the illness is in the mind. But my mind isn't ill, my brain has never hurt.

There's a scandal on the TV because they showed a photo of the policeman's severed head. But it's not because of his hairstyle. This is the scandal: some people think they shouldn't show pictures of severed heads on the TV. Or corpses. Other people think they should, that everyone has a right to see the truth. Yolcaut laughs at this scandal and says that this is the bullshit people amuse themselves with. I don't say anything. But I don't think it's bullshit. Yolcaut thinks it's bullshit because he doesn't care about truth and lies. I was about to tell him that gangs are about telling the truth too, but I kept quiet. What happened is I became a mute. And I also

Down the Rabbit Hole

stopped being called Tochtli. Now I'm called Usagi and I'm a Japanese mute.

It's been barely seven hours since I became a mute and already I'm an enigma and a mystery. Everyone wants to know why I'm not speaking and to stop me being mute. Cinteotl made me a cup of tea with some foul-tasting herbs, supposedly to cure my throat. Yolcaut thinks I'm mute because he hasn't got me the Liberian pygmy hippopotamus and spends all his time telling me I must be patient. But I didn't become mute because of that, it was Yolcaut's lies.

I can't explain why I'm mute to anyone now. Mutes don't give explanations. Or they give them with their hands. I don't know the hand language mutes use, so I'm a mute squared. Mazatzin asked me if we could speak by writing. Then I decided to be deaf, and mute with writing too. To be deaf what you have to do is remember a snatch of a song and repeat it over and over in your head. I picked a little bit from 'The King', where it says Cryyy and cryyy, cryyy and cryyy, cryyy and cryyy, cryyy and cryyy. The writing bit is easier, you just have to be illiterate: instead of writing words you do drawings or rather squiggles. And so now I'm deaf and mute cubed.

Today I'm wearing a Japanese samurai hat. Inside I'm carrying my tiny little pistol with the minuscule bullets. Shhhh . . .

We rabbits do poos like pellets.
Perfect little round pellets, like the ammunition for
    pistols.
We rabbits shoot poo bullets with pistols.

TWO

On the plane on the way to Paris, Franklin Gómez pointed out the French people. The French are like us and don't have two heads or anything like that. That's why they're advanced: because they're like us and even so they invented the guillotine. Whereas we use machetes to cut off heads. The difference between the guillotine and the machete is that the guillotine is devastating. With a guillotine, you can cut off a head in just one slice. Whereas with a machete you have to do lots more slices, at least four. And with the guillotine you can make immaculate cuts, you don't even splatter blood around. By the way, Franklin Gómez started being Franklin Gómez yesterday in the airport. That's what his passport from the country of Honduras says: Franklin Gómez. There were problems because Franklin Gómez didn't want to be Franklin Gómez. Until Winston López convinced him. Franklin Gómez thought this name was suspicious and he wouldn't be allowed to travel. Then Winston López showed him the sport in the newspaper. The day before, Mexico and the country of Honduras had played a football match. In order to convince Franklin Gómez to become Franklin Gómez, Winston López read him out the line-up for Honduras: Astor Henríquez, Maynor Figueroa, Junior Izaguirre, Wilson Palacios, Eddy Vega, Wilmer Velásquez, Milton Núñez . . . Franklin Gómez still wasn't sure, saying that a group of Hondurans travelling to Monrovia would be very suspicious. Then Winston López asked him who in the world gives a fuck about Honduras or Liberia and everything was sorted out.

Winston López told me about ten times that I had to learn the names and I couldn't get it wrong. We are: Winston López, Franklin Gómez and Junior López. If I get it wrong we won't be able to get to Monrovia. But I've got a really good memory, we'll definitely get there. I got to be Junior López, although Franklin Gómez calls me JR. Winston López told him to stop pissing around, but Franklin Gómez thinks that if we're going to get to Monrovia we need to act naturally. You act naturally when you want to be good at lying and cheating. Yolcaut knows a lot about acting naturally: he acts naturally when he says the room with the guns and rifles is empty. But these are things that happened to Tochtli and Usagi, who are mutes, but not to Junior López.

After Paris we have to take two more planes to get to Monrovia. One plane that takes us from Europe to Africa and another that takes us from Africa to Monrovia. Winston López says travelling to Monrovia is as difficult as sailing to Lagos de Moreno. Lagos de Moreno is Miztli's village and it doesn't have lakes or charros. It has lots of priests and a tiny little stinking river that not even a motorboat can get down. Franklin Gómez says getting to Monrovia is as difficult as travelling from one third-world country to another third-world country.

Franklin Gómez has come to Monrovia with us because he can speak French and English. Monrovia is the capital of the country of Liberia where the Liberian pygmy hippopotamuses live and where the Monrovians speak English.

In the plane from Paris, Franklin Gómez spoke French to the French servant girls. And spent the whole journey drinking the French people's champagne. Winston López told him to take advantage of being in first class, which isn't for people dying of hunger like him. The French servant girls on the plane said their 'r's really strangely, as if they had a sore throat or the 'r' was stuck in it. Pathetic. Maybe the French have sore throats because of cutting off their kings' heads.

When we landed in Paris, Franklin Gómez got all excited and said we'd arrived in the land of liberty, fraternity and equality. Apparently the reason you cut off kings' heads is to have those things. Winston López just said:

'Franklin, don't be an asshole.'

The first thing we did in Monrovia was to get a Monrovian guide. Our Monrovian guide is called John Kennedy Johnson and he speaks English to Franklin Gómez. A Monrovian guide is good for three things: so you don't get lost in Monrovia, so you don't get killed in Monrovia, and for finding Liberian pygmy hippopotamuses. That's why he's charging us a lot of money, millions of dollars I think. Because it turns out that finding Liberian pygmy hippopotamuses isn't easy, even in Liberia. John Kennedy Johnson says that Liberian pygmy hippopotamuses are on the edge of extinction. Extinction is when everything dies and it's not just for Liberian pygmy hippopotamuses. Extinction is for all living beings that can die, including Hondurans like us.

The good thing is that when you're on the edge of extinction it's not all of you who are dead, only the majority. But there are very few Liberian pygmy hippopotamuses still alive in Liberia, 1,000 or 2,000 at the most. And there's another problem: they spend their whole lives hidden in the forests. And to top it off they don't live in herds but are solitary and go about two by two or three by three. That's what John Kennedy Johnson's job is, to find animals that are hard to find. John Kennedy Johnson's clients want to hunt the animals. John Kennedy Johnson takes them to where the animals are and the hunters shoot them dead. Then the hunters cut off the animals' heads and take them back home so they can hang them over the mantelpiece in their house. And with the skin they make a mat to wipe their feet on. We don't want to shoot the Liberian pygmy hippopotamuses dead. We just want to capture one or two and take them to live in our palace.

To make the safari go well John Kennedy Johnson advised us to switch around our sleeping patterns. He says it's the best thing if we want to have enough energy to look for the Liberian pygmy hippopotamuses. Switching around your sleeping pattern means sleeping in the day and living at night. The thing is it's easier to find Liberian pygmy hippopotamuses at night, when they come out of their hiding places to look for food. Switching around our sleeping patterns is easy for us, because it means going to sleep after breakfast time in Monrovia, which is the middle of the night in Mexico. And then waking up in the evening in Monrovia, which is the morning in Mexico.

When we wake up, the servants in our hotel, the Mamba Point Hotel, bring food up to our room. They bring: hamburgers, chips, some kind of tough meat and lettuce salads we throw in the bin so we don't get ill with Monrovia's diseases. Lettuce is dangerous. At least that's what Franklin Gómez says, that lettuce transmits diseases. It seems that lettuces are like pigeons, intimate friends of infection. You eat an infected lettuce leaf and you get a devastating disease. Now that I think about it, maybe Quecholli went mute from a disease in that lettuce she likes so much.

Franklin Gómez says John Kennedy Johnson has the name of a president of the United States who was shot dead in the head. President John Kennedy was driving around in a car with no roof and they shot him in the head. So guillotines are for kings and bullets for presidents.

The bad thing about being Junior López is that I can't wear my hats. Winston López says it's to do with not calling attention to ourselves while we're in Monrovia. My hats stayed in our palace, stored in the hat room. It's hot in Monrovia, but

my head was cold, really cold. So Winston López bought me
two African safari hats in the Mamba Point Hotel gift shop.
They're hats that look like aliens' flying saucers. One is khaki
and the other is olive green, which are camouflage colours
for hiding yourself.

African safari hats are hats animal hunters wear and
they're good for looking for Liberian pygmy hippopotamuses.
Actually they're good for looking for any animal, a lion or
even a rhinoceros. They're like detective hats, which are good
for doing investigations, but specialised in animals.

At ten o'clock at night in Monrovia, John Kennedy Johnson comes to pick us up from the Mamba Point Hotel in his
jeep to go on safari. This is what a safari is: you get in a jeep
and you go into the forest, the jungle and the swamps to look
for animals. There are safaris for killing animals and safaris
for catching them. There are also safaris just for looking at
animals. This is to avoid making them go extinct. Winston
López says this is pathetic. As well as the jeep we also have
to use a pickup truck with cages in it to keep the animals in.
Driving the truck is John Kennedy Johnson's partner, who's
called Martin Luther King Taylor. John Kennedy Johnson's
jeep bounces around a lot as we drive along the roads from
Monrovia to the forests of Liberia. It bounces when we drive
into a hole and bounces again when we get out. After that
it gets worse, because in the forests of Liberia there aren't
even any roads. We drive into the trees and the jeep bounces
around so much you can't even feel it bouncing any more.
It's like flying. John Kennedy Johnson has some special headlights to light up the forests of Liberia. We go out looking for

the Liberian pygmy hippopotamuses with these headlights, but we can't find them. So far we've seen: on the first day, antelopes, monkeys and pigs. On the second day, antelopes, vipers and even a leopard. And on the third day, antelopes and monkeys. But zero Liberian pygmy hippopotamuses, zero.

I think the African safari hats I'm wearing are useless, because they're not authentic. It's because we bought them in a gift shop and not a hat shop. All because of Yolcaut's paranoia. If he'd let me bring my detective hats we would've definitely found the Liberian pygmy hippopotamuses by now.

The worst thing is that when we're not on safari we're totally bored. We spend the whole time shut up in the Mamba Point Hotel, because in Monrovia there's nothing nice to look at. We're so bored Franklin Gómez is teaching me all the card games that exist. It would have been better if we'd gone to the empire of Japan. Over there we would have looked for Japanese mutes in the daytime and in cities. But we came to Liberia to look for the Liberian pygmy hippopotamuses, which look like they've gone extinct. Winston López says that to play cards we'd have been better off going to Las Vegas. Fucking shit-hole of a country Liberia.

Franklin Gómez says Martin Luther King Taylor has the name of a man from the country of the United States who was also shot dead. It seems the Liberians really like naming themselves after murdered corpses.

The rum from the country of Liberia comes in these dark bottles, as if it was poison, but it's really good because it stops things being boring. If you drink one glass you feel like laughing and if you drink more you start telling jokes. In the Mamba Point Hotel you can order bottles of rum from the country of Liberia over the phone at any time of day. Even if it's four o'clock in the morning. Today when we got back from looking for the Liberian pygmy hippopotamuses we ordered two bottles.

We still haven't found the Liberian pygmy hippopotamuses, today all we saw were packs of wild dogs. Winston López says if we'd wanted to see stray dogs we could have stayed in Mexico. He started shooting them in sheer rage. The dogs tried to run away but Yolcaut has really good aim. He would've killed them all if Mazatzin hadn't persuaded him to stop shooting, to remember we weren't supposed to be calling attention to ourselves.

The truth is, by now we're sick of looking for the Liberian pygmy hippopotamuses and not finding them. That's why we ordered two bottles of rum from the country of Liberia. Really it was Winston López and Franklin Gómez who ordered them, but they let me come to their party. You drink rum from the country of Liberia with Coca-Cola and ice. This is called a Cuba Libre. You put ice in a glass, and you fill half with rum from the country of Liberia and the other half with Coca-Cola. Franklin Gómez prefers to drink it warm, without ice. He says the ice from the Mamba Point Hotel might have Monrovia's devastating diseases in. Winston López would rather get ill than drink warm Cuba Libres that taste like shit without ice.

Winston López's jokes are about Spaniards, who are really ridiculous people: it takes three Spaniards to change a light-bulb. The Spaniards nearly always get muddled up and come to strange conclusions. Then there are the jokes about countries that all start the same: there was a Mexican, a Gringo and a Russian. The Russian might change, sometimes it's a Spaniard, or a Frenchman, or a German. When there was a Russian in the joke, Franklin Gómez said that the joke was old, because the Russians aren't Communists any more. Winston López just said:

'Franklin, don't be an asshole.'

The good thing is that later he stopped being such an asshole. At least that's what Winston López says, that when Franklin Gómez gets drunk he stops being such an asshole.

The joke I liked best was the one about some Mexican policemen who made a hippopotamus confess it was a rabbit. It wasn't a Liberian pygmy hippopotamus, just a normal hippopotamus. The joke was about a competition between the policemen in the FBI from the country of the United States, the KGB from the country of Russia, and the Mexican police, to see who would be the first to find a pink rabbit in the forest. In the end the Mexican policemen turned up with a hippopotamus painted pink saying:

'I'm a rabbit, I'm a rabbit.'

This was funny, but it was also a little bit true. That's why I liked this joke so much: because it wasn't really a joke. Everyone knows pink rabbits don't really exist.

The good thing about the edge of extinction is that it's not extinction yet. Today we finally found the Liberian pygmy hippopotamuses. And I wasn't even wearing a hat. My head was bare and I was taking the cold like a man. There were two Liberian pygmy hippopotamuses and their ears were just how I imagined them: minuscule like the bullets from a tiny little gun. When we saw them they were in a muddy swamp eating the weeds. They were such nice animals to look at, as if they were the children of a pig and a walrus. Or a pig and a manatee. John Kennedy Johnson shot them with a special rifle with sleeping bullets. The bullets from this rifle are injections with a poisonous substance that puts animals to sleep so you can capture them. The injection got one of the Liberian pygmy hippopotamuses in the back. It got the other one in the neck. After a few seconds the Liberian pygmy hippopotamuses lay down on their sides and fell asleep. John Kennedy Johnson, Martin Luther King Taylor, Franklin Gómez and Winston López lifted them into the cages in the back of the pickup truck. Even though they're pygmies they weigh lots of kilograms, easily more than 1,000, which is a tonne. Then we bounced all the way back to the Mamba Point Hotel in the jeep. Our pygmy hippopotamuses were taken to the port of Monrovia to be put on a pirate ship to go to Mexico. But they'll take a long time to get there, four months or more. Because you can't go straight from the port of Monrovia to the port of Veracruz. You have to stop in lots of cities before you get to Mexico.

We're going to leave soon, too. Winston López ordered Franklin Gómez to investigate what had happened in Mexico over the last few days, to look for some news about a man called El Amarillo. Franklin Gómez went to use the Mamba

Point Hotel's computer and when he came back he just said:

'Uh-huh.' And Winston López laughed in a really strange way.

I think this means we can leave now.

The most important thing now is that our Liberian pygmy hippopotamuses arrive safely in Mexico. That's why we have to plan everything scrupulously and give detailed instructions. The bales of alfalfa our Liberian pygmy hippopotamuses will eat during the journey must be immaculate, with no infections. I calculate each hippo will eat a bale a day, or more. We've also given orders for them to be fed apples and grapes, which they really like. I made a list: twenty apples and thirty bunches of grapes a day. Per head. Mix up the alfalfa, apples and grapes to make gigantic salads.

Franklin Gómez translated the list of instructions into English and we gave it to John Kennedy Johnson so he can give it to the pirates. John Kennedy Johnson says we were really lucky, because we caught a male and a female. The list also says they should wash our Liberian pygmy hippopotamuses three times a week and clean their minuscule ears. Speaking of food, Azcatl's going to be happy when he sees our Liberian pygmy hippopotamuses, because they'll help him get rid of the weeds in the garden of our palace.

Franklin Gómez asked me if I'd thought of any names for our Liberian pygmy hippopotamuses yet. This was a secret I hadn't told anyone, not even Miztli, who's really good at keeping secrets. I thought if I told anyone it would be bad luck and I'd never have a Liberian pygmy hippopotamus. The problem was I'd only thought of one name. I hadn't thought of two names, because I didn't think I'd have two Liberian pygmy hippopotamuses. Now it wasn't just about choosing another name. The two names had to sound good together. So I spent ages thinking, making combinations, and writing them all down in a list.

In the end I chose the names I still liked after repeating them 100 times. It's a foolproof test. You repeat something 100 times and if you still like it it's because it's good. This doesn't just work for names, it works for anything, food or people. Franklin Gómez thought they were really odd names to give Liberian pygmy hippopotamuses. Cinteotl says odd-ness is related to ugliness. But they're not ugly names or odd ones, they're names you don't get tired of saying 100 times or more. Winston López is right. Educated people know a lot about books, but they don't know anything about life. There's no book that tells you how to choose names for Liberian pygmy hippopotamuses. Most books are about useless things that don't matter to anyone.

Today we went to look around Monrovia. All because Winston López was in a good mood and hired a 4x4. It was the first time I saw the city in the daytime and I discovered that Liberia isn't really a disastrous country. It's a sordid country. It smelled of fried fish and burnt oil everywhere. And there were lots of people in the street, too, thousands of people or more. They were people who weren't doing anything, they were just sitting around or talking and laughing. The houses were really ugly. Monrovia is not an immaculate city like Orlando, where we went on holiday once. Franklin Gómez says Monrovia looks like Poza Rica, but I don't know if that's true because I've never been to Poza Rica. I'd say it looks like La Chona.

As there wasn't anything nice to see we started looking for bullet holes in the walls as we drove around. In the country of Liberia there was a war not very long ago. It seems incredible but it was fun: we invented a game, the game of seeing who could find the wall with the most bullet holes in it. Franklin Gómez found the wall of a shop with sixteen bullet holes in it. I found one on a house with loads more, twenty-three. In any case Winston López won, and he was driving. Winston López's wall was on a school and it had ninety-eight bullet holes in it. We managed to count them one by one because we got out of the 4x4. Franklin Gómez started to take photos while giving a lecture about injustice. He talked about the rich and the poor, about Europe and Africa, about wars, hunger and diseases. And about whose fault it is: the French people's, who like cutting off kings' heads so much, and the Spanish, who don't like cutting off kings' heads, and the Portuguese, who love selling African people, and the English and the Gringos, who actually prefer to make corpses with bombs. Franklin Gómez went on and on with his lecture. Winston López took his camera away and said:

'Don't be an asshole, Franklin, we don't do that.' Then we went to buy souvenirs from Liberia. I bought five genuine African safari hats in a special safari shop. The hats are all the same shape, but they're different colours. One's grey, one's olive green, one's coffee-coloured, one's white and one's khaki. Winston López bought some figurines of African men from a local handicrafts shop and also two decorative masks to hang on the walls of our palace. And some African jewels that must be for Quecholli. We paid for all these things with our dollars and we could have bought loads more, because we have millions of dollars. But we didn't buy more things because they wouldn't fit in our suitcases. Unlike us Franklin Gómez bought souvenirs that don't need to go in a suitcase: two years of school for four Liberian girls, ten vaccines for Liberian babies and twenty books for Monrovia's public library. We had to go to an office to do all that. While Franklin Gómez was filling in a big pile of forms they'd given him, Winston López said something enigmatic to me. He said:

'Look at him, he's a saint.'

When we got back to the hotel Franklin Gómez had an expression like you couldn't tell if he was laughing or about to cry. At least now he was really quiet, looking at some certificates he'd been given by the people in the office he bought his souvenirs from. Winston López just said:

'Franklin, you really are a total asshole.'

This is the most disastrous day of my whole life. And nothing was supposed to have happened, because the only thing we were going to do was wait until tomorrow to go to the airport and fly home to Mexico. But in the afternoon John Kennedy Johnson turned up and started to talk about secret things with Franklin Gómez. Then we all went to the port of Monrovia to visit our Liberian pygmy hippopotamuses.

In the port of Monrovia we walked past cranes and gigantic crates until we got to an abandoned warehouse. Martin Luther King Taylor was standing in the doorway of the warehouse with a rifle. Before we went in Winston López told me there was a problem, that our Liberian pygmy hippopotamuses were ill. He tried to go into the warehouse on his own but I wouldn't let him, I said that gangs are about not hiding things and about seeing the truth. Winston López ordered Franklin Gómez to stay and wait with me outside and not to let me in. So I kicked him three times and said he was a lousy lying piece of shit, and that I knew he was lying about the room with the guns and rifles. Winston López stroked my head with his ringless fingers and said it was all right, and we all went in together.

The warehouse stank. Franklin Gómez said it was because of the Liberian pygmy hippopotamuses' shit. Inside it was quite dark, because there weren't any windows and the only light came in through a gap between the walls and the aluminium roof. It was better that way. The walls were disgusting, with the paint peeling off in chunks, and wherever you walked you stepped in things that made a strange noise. Right at the end were the cages with our Liberian pygmy hippopotamuses. I asked which one was the male and which one the female and John Kennedy Johnson said the male was the one on the right, which was bigger than the one on the left. But this didn't matter now, because they weren't nice animals to look at any more. They were both lying down with their eyes closed and they weren't even moving. They were really dirty and there was blood and shit everywhere. John Kennedy Johnson told us not to go near them or they'd get scared.

We were looking at our Liberian pygmy hippopotamuses when I realised that Itzcuauhtli should have come to Monrovia with us too. If Itzcuauhtli had come he would have given them the right medicine to make them better. Then Louis XVI started to writhe around and make horrible squealing sounds. It was a horrible sound because you heard it and you wanted to be dead so you wouldn't have to hear it. He squealed really loudly, so loudly you couldn't hear anything else, not even the noises from the port or the voices of everyone in the warehouse. When he was quiet at last, Franklin Gómez told us that John Kennedy Johnson said the best thing would be to put down our Liberian pygmy hippopotamuses, so they didn't suffer.

Winston López took me aside and repeated what John Kennedy Johnson had just told us. He promised me we'd get some more Liberian pygmy hippopotamuses and he even forgot that I was Junior López and he was Winston López when he said:

'Tochtli, remember: Yolcaut always finds a way.'

Then he asked me to go out of the warehouse with Franklin Gómez. I didn't want to, because I'm a macho man, and macho men aren't afraid. And anyway, gangs are about not hiding things and about seeing the truth. Then Winston López gave John Kennedy Johnson the order: to kill our Liberian pygmy hippopotamuses. Franklin Gómez tried to protest that I shouldn't watch, he told Winston López not to be cruel, and said I was too young to see a thing like that. Winston López just ordered him to shut his fucking trap.

Martin Luther King Taylor went up to the cages armed with his rifle. First he went over to the cage on the right and held the weapon to Louis XVI's heart. The sound of the bullet went bouncing around the walls of the warehouse together with the horrible squeals of the Liberian pygmy hippopotamus. But the one crying was Marie Antoinette of Austria, who was frightened by the noise. Louis XVI was already dead. My legs started to shake. We waited until Marie Antoinette stopped squealing and then Martin Luther King Taylor did the same with her. Except she didn't die with one shot. She was moving around and the bullet didn't hit her right in the heart. She didn't stop moving until the fourth shot. Then it turned out I'm not macho after all and I started to cry like a faggot. I also wet my pants. I squealed horribly as if I was a Liberian pygmy hippopotamus who wanted the people listening to want to be dead so they didn't have to hear me. I wanted them to put eight bullets in my prostate to make me into a corpse. And I wanted the whole world to be extinct. Franklin Gómez came over to give me a hug but Winston López shouted at him to leave me alone.

When I calmed down, I had a really strange feeling in my chest. It was hot and it didn't hurt, but it made me think I was the most pathetic person in the whole universe.

THREE

We Japanese cut off heads with sabres, which are special swords that have the same devastating blade as guillotines. The advantage of sabres over guillotines is that with sabres you can also cut off arms, legs, noses, ears, hands or whatever you like. Also you can cut people in half. Whereas with guillotines you can only cut off heads. The truth is not all Japanese people use sabres. That would be like saying all Mexicans wear charro sombreros. It's only Japanese samurai like me who use sabres.

The samurai in films do battle for honour and loyalty. We'd rather die than be faggots. Like in the film *The Fugitive Samurai*. It's about a samurai who runs away to save another samurai's honour. But he only runs away for a bit, because what he really wants is revenge. Samurai are like gangs, which are about solidarity and protection. Then one day the fugitive samurai stops being a fugitive because he goes back to the other samurai's house by skiing down a snow-capped mountain. This is my favourite bit in the film. On his way the samurai who was once a fugitive meets all the enemies who wanted to kill him. And the samurai who was a fugitive chops them all up into little bits with his sword. Some he just cuts off an arm or a leg. Others he cuts off their head. And he cuts lots of them in half. All the snow is slowly stained with the enemies' blood, as if it was a blackcurrant or strawberry Slush Puppie.

At the end of the film the samurai who was a fugitive discovers that the other samurai whose honour he wanted to save was already a corpse. The samurai who was a fugitive takes a knife and sticks it in himself so he becomes a corpse too. We Japanese don't need happy endings in films. We're not like the charros, who need women and love and always end up singing like they're so happy. And such faggots.

To be a samurai you have to wear a dressing gown over your clothes and put on a samurai hat. Samurai hats are like giant upside down pozole bowls. You have to hide your sword in your dressing gown. I don't have a samurai sword yet, but I'm going to ask Miztli for one. Yolcaut definitely won't want him to buy me one. That's why this time as well as the list of things I want I made a list of the secret things I want. Only Miztli and I will know about it. Miztli will understand. Yolcaut doesn't understand anything, he hasn't even realised I'm a samurai. He wants me to take off the dressing gown and says I can't spend the whole day dressed like this, that I look like a little rich kid. And he thinks I'm mute because of what happened to our Liberian pygmy hippopotamuses. Cinteotl and Itzpapalotl don't understand anything either.

Whenever they see me they tell me to take off my pyjamas.

Mazatzin is the only one who's happy and he's giving me special classes about things from the empire of Japan. Today he told me about the Second World War. It was to do with two cities from the empire of Japan that were destroyed with atomic bombs. If someone fires an atomic bomb at you a samurai sword doesn't do any good. As he told this story Mazatzin grew less and less happy and ended up giving one of his lectures. This one was about war, the economy and imperialists. And he kept saying:

'The Gringos, Usagi, the lousy fucking Gringos.'

Today Paul Smith, who hasn't been to our palace for a really long time, about three months, came round. I found out I actually know fifteen people and not fourteen or fifteen. The thing is I wasn't sure if Paul Smith was still a person or if by now he was a corpse. I had my doubts because of one of Yolcaut's enigmatic phrases, which he said when I asked him once why Paul Smith didn't come round any more:

'If he's smart he'll come back, if he's an asshole he won't.'

Paul Smith is Yolcaut's partner in his business with the country of the United States and he's got really strange hair. Actually the strange hair is the hair on his toupee, the rest of it is normal. But the hair on the toupee is disgusting. Yolcaut says Paul Smith has hair transplants because he's going bald. He has to pay millions of dollars for every hair they put on his head. Paul Smith really is the most ridiculous person I know.

Mazatzin doesn't like Paul Smith either. Whenever he sees him he says:

'Hey, Gringo, have you guys invaded a country in the last twenty minutes?'

And Paul Smith replies:

'Your fucking mother, you naco, we invaded your fucking mother.'

Paul Smith pronounces his 'r's really strangely too, but not like the French, who sound as if their throats hurt from cutting off so many kings' heads. Paul Smith says his 'r's as if he thinks he's really important. It's an arrogant man's 'r' that echoes around inside his mouth. It's to do with being a Gringo, arrogant people who think they own the world. At least that's what Mazatzin says in his lectures.

As well as sorting out their business deals, there's always a party when Paul Smith comes. At these parties Paul Smith goes to the bathroom a lot. At first I thought that Paul Smith must have a small bladder, but then Miztli told me a secret, he said it was so he could take cocaine. You take cocaine with your nose and in secret, in the bathroom or inside a cupboard. That's why it's such a good business, because it's secret.

Paul Smith doesn't understand anything about samurai either. He asked me if I was ill because I was walking around in a dressing gown. I'm not ill and what's more: since I've been a samurai my tummy doesn't hurt. Well, it does hurt, but I concentrate like the Japanese and it stops hurting. When Yolcaut told him I hadn't said a thing for three days, Paul Smith started saying Let's see if being mute is contagious. Paul Smith is an asshole. Since I've been mute there are more mysterious things. Is Paul Smith clever and is that why he came back? He can't be, with his hair transplants and his ridiculous ideas Paul Smith can't be clever. He's definitely an asshole. But I can't ask Yolcaut, no way. This enigma will remain unsolved. Mutes don't ask for explanations or give explanations. Mutes are all about silence.

Since we came back from Monrovia severed heads have gone out of fashion. Now it's more human remains they show on TV. Sometimes it's a nose, other times it's a windpipe or an intestine. Ears too. It can be anything apart from heads and hands. That's what makes them human remains and not corpses. With corpses you can tell who the people were before they turned into corpses. While with human remains you can't tell who the people were.

Human remains aren't kept in baskets or crates of vintage brandy but in plastic bags from the supermarket, as if you could buy human remains in the supermarket. At the most you can buy cow, pig or chicken remains in the supermarket. I think if they sold severed heads in the supermarket people would use them to make pozole. But first you'd have to take off their hair, just like you take the feathers off chickens. Bald people like me would be more expensive, because we'd already be ready to go in the pozole.

Before I went to bed Yolcaut gave me a present. It was a Gringo cowboy hat, the kind they wear for lassoing cows. Then he said that cowboys don't go around in dressing gowns. As I didn't reply, not even a thank you, he shouted:

'Speak, motherfucker, will you stop with this bullshit!'

I think he wanted to hit me, but he didn't hit me, because Yolcaut's never hit me. Instead of hitting me Yolcaut gives me presents. These are all the presents Yolcaut has given me to stop me being mute: the new Playstation, which is the Playstation 3, with six different games; some cowboy chaps, as if I liked chaps or cowboys; a cage with three hamsters; a fish tank with two turtles; food for the hamsters and food for the turtles; a wheel for the hamsters; some stones and a plastic palm tree for the turtles' fish tank. Presents don't stop me being mute, no way. And I won't stop being a Japanese samurai just because Yolcaut wants me to be a cowboy like Paul Smith.

The most mysterious thing they've done to try to stop me being mute was in the morning, when Cinteotl and Itzpapalotl turned up for work. They weren't alone, they had two little boys with them: a cousin of Cinteotl's and a neighbour of Itzpapalotl's. They both had awful haircuts, like soldiers, who have the worst haircuts in the universe. Yolcaut didn't let the boys stay, as much as Cinteotl and Itzpapalotl kept saying I needed friends my own age, that it was to stop me being mute. They also said it wasn't normal for me to be walking around in a dressing gown and wearing those odd hats I like so much. Yolcaut got fed up with them and just said:

'You can shut up or clear off.'

And he ordered Miztli to take the boys back home. One of them, the one that was Itzpapalotl's neighbour, came over to me before he left and gave me a toy he'd brought with him. Pathetic, although Itzpapalotl told him he was a very good boy. It was a Star Wars figure, but it wasn't an original, it was a fake one from the market. It wasn't even painted properly. The doll was supposed to have red clothes and flesh-coloured skin. Well, a bit of his right hand was actually painted red. And it wasn't blood. It was just that the doll was cheap. When they'd left I threw it in the rubbish bin.

This really is mysterious: the minuscule bullets from the tiny little pistol do make corpses. Maybe not human corpses, and not corpses of big animals either, but corpses of small animals at least. I didn't mean to kill the lovebird, I wanted to see what the birds would do when they heard the sound of the bullets. What happened was after the first shot all the parakeets and lovebirds started flying around as if they'd gone mad. They crashed into the walls of the cage and attacked each other as if one of them was doing the shooting. Coloured feathers started flying around everywhere. There were red ones, blue ones, green ones, yellow ones, white ones, black ones and grey ones. Then I shot twice more, aiming at the feathers. The problem was that inside the cage there was a lot of confusion. It was when the parakeets and lovebirds calmed down and went back into their houses and to their branches that I discovered the lovebird's corpse on the ground. It was a sky-blue lovebird, although it wasn't really a lovebird any more, because it was dead and the dead are not lovebirds. The minuscule bullet had made the blood come out of one of its wings.

Before anyone came I hid the tiny little pistol in the weeds in the garden. I threw it as far as I could into a part where the undergrowth is so high Azcatl doesn't even bother cutting it back any more. Itzcuauhtli came over to the cage and started looking at the mess of feathers and the lovebird's corpse. This was the most mysterious and enigmatic thing I've ever seen in my life. How did he hear the shots if he's a deaf mute? Itzcuauhtli went into the cage and picked up the lovebird's corpse from the floor. As he saw it was already dead he didn't even go and get the medicine to make it better. The good thing is that since he's a deaf mute and I'm a mute we stood there in silence and he didn't ask me for an explanation. But that's when Cinteotl and Itzpapalotl arrived and when they saw the corpse they started saying Oh my goodness, poor little thing, how could someone kill a lovebird that never hurt anyone and all it does is give kisses to other lovebirds. They also said that because of me one of the lovebirds had been left a widow and they'd have to find it another mate so it didn't die of sadness. And they went to Yolcaut and told on me.

Yolcaut didn't care about the lovebird's life, because he didn't make a fuss like Cinteotl and Itzpapalotl did. Lovebirds are faggots. Anyway we've still got lots of lovebirds left, seven. The thing Yolcaut cared about was knowing which gun I'd killed the lovebird with and where the gun was and where I'd got the gun from. But since I'm a mute and mutes don't give explanations I didn't tell him anything, I stayed quiet. Yol-caut locked himself up with Miztli in the room with the guns and rifles and I felt like asking them what they were plan-ning on doing locked in an empty room. Later on Yolcaut and Miztli had an argument because they discovered there was a pistol missing, the tiny little pistol with the minuscule bul-lets. Yolcaut blamed Miztli for having left the room with the guns and rifles unlocked. Miztli said Yolcaut's paranoia was to blame, because without Yolcaut's paranoia it wouldn't be necessary to keep the guns loaded. The truth is, it's Miztli's fault, because he hasn't bought me a samurai sword.

Mazatzin also got annoyed with me, but he didn't get annoyed because I made the lovebird into a corpse or because I stole the tiny little pistol. He got annoyed because in order to make a samurai sword you need a 1,000-year-old tradition and lots of patience. While to make pistols you only need the factories of the capitalists.

'Who do you think you are,' Mazatzin asked, 'the Cow-boy Mouse?'

But the Cowboy Mouse had two pistols. And my ears are bigger. My ears are so big they always get cut off in photos.

On the TV there's a new theory about the human remains: before, they thought the human remains were from several corpses, and with the new theory they think they're really only from one corpse. This is because they found several pieces of evidence and one clue. The evidence is that none of the body parts have turned up more than once, they're always different. They're doing some tests in the lab to find out whether it's just one corpse. The clue is that they found a piece of flesh from the back. And the piece of flesh had a tattoo of a tiny blue unicorn. The truth is, you couldn't see a unicorn on the TV at all, just a mark. Then something mysterious happened. Yolcaut sent for Miztli, even though it was night-time and it was Miztli's turn to guard the palace. And when Miztli arrived, Yolcaut ordered him to go and get Quecholli. But Quecholli didn't come, or if she came she left really soon, because when I woke up in the morning she wasn't there.

Then what happened was that Mazatzin didn't come to give me my lessons, and today isn't even Saturday or Sunday. It got to nine o'clock, half past nine, ten, still no sign of him. He didn't come. That's never happened. Maybe Mazatzin doesn't want to come any more because he's disappointed I'm not a real samurai. This isn't my fault, because I can't be a real samurai without a sword. Yolcaut told me to go and get my books and study, as if Mazatzin was here. But I went and played on the Playstation 3, taking advantage of the fact that Yolcaut left the palace with Miztli and was out all day. Chichilkuali stayed to guard the palace, except instead of guarding the palace he guarded me. He followed me around really closely all day long, like Quecholli does with Yolcaut. He even stood outside waiting for me when I went to the toilet.

In the evening, Yolcaut and Miztli came back to the palace. Yolcaut wouldn't let me watch TV with him. He pretended nothing was wrong and sent me away with Miztli to distract me. Anyway now I know why Yolcaut didn't want me to watch TV. Miztli told me, because Miztli is really good at secrets. What I mean is Miztli's really good if you want to find out secrets, and really bad if you want him to keep them. And you don't even have to say a thing to him. What normally happens is that to find out secrets you have to ask lots of times or even give people devastating blows to make them tell you. But not with Miztli. As I'm a mute I didn't ask him anything but even so he told me that they're talking about Yolcaut on the TV, about Yolcaut's business. Although they don't actually call him Yolcaut, they call him the King. Miztli says that now we're really in the shit. He says:

'Just think, he won't even let you watch TV any more. Get ready, now the paranoia's really going to start.'

I thought Yolcaut's paranoia had been around for a while and now it looks like it's only just started. In the dictionary it says that to be paranoid you have to think about just one thing. That is, paranoid people are mad. It's as if I only thought about hats. But I think about lots of things: hats, samurai, swords, Liberian pygmy hippopotamuses, lettuce, tiny little pistols with minuscule bullets, guillotines, the French, bullets, corpses, hair transplants... Just for the sake of thinking I even think about the Spanish, and they don't even like cutting off kings' heads. The thing is, I'm not paranoid. Who knows what it is Yolcaut thinks about all the time?

I knew it, I knew it: Mazatzin isn't a saint at all, he's a pathetic traitor. He's written an article in a magazine where he reveals all our secrets, our enemies and our mysteries. The article has photos of our palace and the title is: 'Down The King's Rabbit Hole'. It talks about our millions of pesos, our millions of dollars, our millions of euros, the gold and diamond rings the King wears, the guns and rifles, Miztli and Chichilkuali, the politicians, even Quecholli. And on the cover there's a photo of our tigers' cage.

The magazine doesn't say the author is Mazatzin, but it's him, we know it is. It can't be anyone else. He hasn't come to give me my lessons for two days. And the name at the end of the article is Chimalli, which means shield. And the meaning of names is very important to Mazatzin, that's why he used to call me Usagi and not Tochtli. That's also why he doesn't call Yolcaut Yolcaut in the article, but the King, like they call him on the TV. Shields are for protection. In other words, Mazatzin must have given himself a name to protect himself because he's scared of Yolcaut.

I know about the article because of Miztli, because Yolcaut doesn't tell me anything. It's as if he's gone mute as well, mute just with me. He talks to other people. Actually he talks to everyone to give orders. I think he's tired of giving me presents to stop me being mute now, and as I haven't stopped being mute he must be taking his revenge. Gangs aren't about revenge, and they're not about lies or hiding the truth either. At this rate we won't be the best gang for eight kilometres any more. In fact, we won't be a gang at all.

The thing with the article meant I stopped being mute just a bit because I had to talk to Miztli. It was to find out what it said in the magazine and to ask him what was going to happen to Mazatzin. By the way, Mazatzin didn't write anything about me, he pretended I didn't exist. Miztli thinks it was to protect me. Pathetic. I'm a samurai and we samurai don't need anyone to protect us. At the most we might need another samurai to protect us, especially when our honour is in danger. But a samurai never needs a pathetic traitor to protect him.

In any case Mazatzin wanting to protect me is useless. Because no one's going to read his article. I used to think the only thing you could kidnap was people. Well it turns out it's not, you can kidnap other things too, like magazines. That's what Yolcaut did when he found out about the article. He phoned up and gave orders to buy up all the magazines with Mazatzin's article in them. Miztli says that Chichilkuali went to a factory where they do recycling: all the magazines will be put in a machine and the machine will turn them into paper for wrapping tortillas in. Poor Mazatzin, Miztli says he'd do well to go very far away. I think Mazatzin's gone to the empire of Japan. Yolcaut's definitely going to drop at least four atomic bombs on him.

Yolcaut really is a paranoid madman. First he went mute with me and wouldn't let me watch TV and now he's shouting at me to run, come quick, Mazatzin's on the TV. I've got a theory: educated people go to jail because they're really idiots. Like Mazatzin, who's not only a traitor to us but it turns out is also a traitor to the country of Honduras. In the country of Honduras forging official documents is a serious crime. Crime: it's a nice word. It turns out the Hondurans are nationalists and they get annoyed if someone tries to be a fake Honduran. If you want a Honduran passport there are two options: you're either a real Honduran or you go to jail.

The worst thing for Mazatzin is that the men from the government of the country of Honduras think he's made fun of the country of Honduras. That's what the vice-president said, that he also made fun of them by trying to use the ridiculous name of Franklin Gómez. The vice-president was called Elvis Martínez. I think only idiots flee to the country of Honduras with a fake Honduran passport. Mazatzin was caught going through the centre of Tegucigalpa, which is the capital of the country of Honduras, a country that's only for real Hondurans.

A man from the government of Mexico said they couldn't do anything for Mazatzin, that Mexico respected the sovereignty of our brothers in the country of Honduras. Are Mexicans and Hondurans brothers? Politicians really do make complicated deals. Yolcaut was really enjoying himself laughing at Mazatzin when he decided to say one of his enigmatic phrases. He said:

'Think the worst and you'll be right.'

And he carried on laughing like a paranoid madman who only thinks about one thing, about laughing.

Not only was this phrase not really enigmatic at all, but it also helped me to solve other mysteries. In other words, this phrase means that what's happening is Yolcaut's fault. That's what the orders are for, to organise the enigmas. But then a very enigmatic thing really did happen: there was a news report on the TV about Mazatzin's life and they were saying he was dangerous. All because he'd gone to live very far away, in the middle of nowhere, on top of a mountain covered with rebel Indians who wanted to shoot the men from the government dead. That's why Mazatzin went to the country of Honduras too, to organise the Indians of the country of Honduras to kill the men from the government of the country of Honduras. Now the government of the country of Honduras has a long list of crimes that will put Mazatzin in jail for many years. Yolcaut says at least twenty-five. And he laughs again. After the news report the people on TV rang up the man who'd been Mazatzin's partner in his advertising business and he said he hadn't seen him for two years, since he went to live on the mountain with the guerrillas. That was the mysterious thing, because Mazatzin wasn't with the guerrillas. He was with us teaching me things from books.

If I was Mazatzin I'd have fled to the empire of Japan. And over there I would have ordered a sword to be made for me so I could be a real samurai. Instead he went to the country of Honduras, and now because of him my fingers really hurt from playing on the Playstation 3 so much.

Today I met the sixteenth person I know and her name is Alotl. According to Cinteotl, Alotl's bottom is this big: two metres. Alotl isn't a herbivore like Quecholli, because she doesn't just eat salads with lettuce, she also eats alphabet soup and enchiladas and meat. And she's not mute, just the opposite, she says lots of things. She says:

'Little man, don't you think it's a bit late to be walking

around dressed like that? This is not the time to be wearing a dressing gown.'

She also says to Cinteotl and Itzpapalotl:

'What a big house and how lovely it is, and what good taste you have, such pretty vases!'

Because she doesn't know this isn't really a house, it's a palace. If she knew it was a palace she'd realise that it isn't really a very good palace, because it's not immaculate. The vases she's talking about are the Chinese vases in the living room with the armchairs. The vases have dragons on them breathing fire from their snouts and the truth is they are pretty. And later, out on the terrace, she said:

'Oh, a tiger in a cage, so big and so beautiful, what good taste to have a tiger in the garden!'

Then the tiger roared. I think the tiger wanted to eat her. She didn't realise, she just said Oh oh oh, what a fierce little kitty, and asked me if the tiger had a name.

Alotl talked so much I was embarrassed to carry on being a mute, because she kept asking me about the dressing gown, about the samurai hat, about the animals' names and saying how did I get to be so handsome? And she was always stroking my head and laughing and saying Oh, oh, oh, the little mute. I had to explain to her about the samurai and why I'm a samurai and how I need a sword to be a real samurai. She also made me show her my collection of hats. She's a nationalist, because the hats she liked best were the charro sombreros, even though I showed her all my three-cornered hats and my authentic safari hats.

When we sat down to eat on the terrace it wasn't an enigmatic moment like before, because Alotl spent the whole time talking about her village and making jokes. Her village is in the north, in Sinaloa. I think Yolcaut liked Alotl, because he even asked her questions and laughed at her jokes. The jokes were about how good-looking Yolcaut and I are and how much we look like each other, just as handsome. Alotl made the names of everyone at the table with her alphabet soup, but she wrote ours like this: 'toshtli' and 'llolcau'.

The good thing was that Alotl didn't spend the whole day going on and on, because she disappeared a lot with Yolcaut, four times. Miztli was also surprised they disappeared so many times and he was happy because he was the one who'd brought Alotl to the palace. When I asked him why they were disappearing so much he laughed and told me a secret, something super-enigmatic:

'Thirty-six, twenty-four, perfect score, Tochtli, thirty-six, twenty-four, perfect score.'

Now Alotl comes every day and not just two or three times a week. One day as a present she brought me a straw hat with a ribbon on it with a picture of a palm tree that says: *Souvenir from Acapulco*. Another day she was wearing a skirt that was so short Cinteotl didn't want to serve her any food. The truth is, the straw hat from Acapulco is the worst hat in my collection, I'd throw it away if it was up to me. The problem is I feel sorry for Yolcaut, who was really pleased with the present. And the skirt really was very short, so short that twice I managed to see her knickers, which were yellow.

The best day of all was the day Alotl brought a samurai film I hadn't seen. She said it was to show me that real samurai don't wear dressing gowns. We even made a bet: if I won she'd buy me a samurai costume and if she won I'd stop wearing the dressing gown. It turned out that some of the samurai were wearing dressing gowns and others weren't, because they were wearing trousers and armour on their chests. Yolcaut said the dressing gown the samurai wore wasn't a checked one like mine. Theirs were black. So they stopped the film and we didn't carry on watching it until I'd taken off the dressing gown.

Anyway, we had a lot of fun watching the film, especially the part with the fights. We also had fun watching the part with the conversations, because the samurai didn't speak Japanese, but a funny kind of Spanish. Yolcaut said they spoke like Spaniards and started calling me what one samurai had been calling one of the baddies: rascal.

At the end of the film one samurai cut off the head of another samurai who was his best friend. He wasn't a traitor, it was the opposite. He did it because they were friends and he wanted to save his honour. Then I don't know what got into Yolcaut because when the film was over he took me into the room with the guns and rifles. He told me that there weren't any secrets between us and let me look at all the weapons and explained what their names were, the countries where they'd been made and the calibres.

For pistols we have Berettas from the country of Italy, Brownings from the kingdom of United and lots from the country of the United States: mainly Colts and Smith &

Wessons. By the way, you can put a silencer on the guns, to make them mute. The rifles are nearly all the same. We have some called AK-47s, from the country of Russia, and other ones called M-16, from the country of the United States. Although we've mostly got Uzis from the country of Israel. Yolcaut also showed me the name of the rifle with the gigantic bullets, which isn't really a rifle, it's a weapon called a bazooka.

Before I went to bed Yolcaut asked me if I'd paid attention to the samurai film and if I'd understood the ending properly. I said I had. Then he said the most enigmatic and mysterious thing he's ever said to me. He said:

'One day you'll have to do the same for me.'

Today when I woke up there was a really big wooden box next to my bed. It had lots of stickers and labels on it that said: FRAGILE and HANDLE WITH CARE. I ran to ask Yolcaut what it was and to ask him to help me open it, because it was nailed shut.

We opened the box and inside there were lots of little polystyrene balls, thousands. I started taking them out until I found the stuffed heads of Louis XVI and Marie Antoinette of Austria, our Liberian pygmy hippopotamuses. The truth is, the people who stuffed them had done a very immaculate job. The severed heads have their snouts open so you can see their tongues and their four tusks. And they're shiny, because they've been varnished with clear paint. Their eyes are made of white marbles with a brown pupil. And their minuscule ears are intact. Their necks are attached to a board that has a little golden plaque with their names. Louis XVI's head, which is a very big head, says LOUIS XVI. And underneath: *Choeropsis liberiensis*. Marie Antoinette of Austria's head, which is a smaller head, says: MARIE ANTOINETTE. And it also says: *Choeropsis liberiensis*.

Together Yolcaut and I hung the heads on the wall in my bedroom: Louis XVI on the right and Marie Antoinette of Austria on the left. Really it was Yolcaut who put the nails in and arranged the heads. I just told him if they were wonky or straight. Then I got up on a chair and tried lots of different hats on them. The ones that look best are the African safari hats. So I left the African safari hats on them, but I'll only leave them there for a bit. Soon the gold and diamond crowns we ordered to be made for them will get here.

On the day of the coronation, me and my dad will have a party.

GLOSSARY

p.3 & throughout: Tochtli – his name means 'rabbit' in Nahuatl, Mexico's main indigenous language (and Usagi is
Japanese for rabbit). All the characters, apart from Cinteotl
the cook, have Nahuatl names that translate as some sort
of animal: Yolcaut means rattlesnake; Mazatzin, deer; Miztli, puma; Quecholli, flamingo; Chichilkuali, red eagle; Itzpapalotl, black butterfly; Itzcuauhtli, white eagle; and Alotl,
macaw.

p.14: pozole – a traditional Mexican soup or stew of pre-
Colombian origin, generally prepared with maize, pork and
chilli. According to research by Mexican and Spanish academ-
ics, the original recipe included the flesh of human sacrifices
on special occasions. This was banned after the Spanish conquest.

p.15: tacos *al pastor* – literally 'shepherd-style tacos', this is a very popular Mexican version of the Middle Eastern street snack of spit-roasted meat, probably brought over by Lebanese immigrants. Similar to the Turkish döner kebab, it consists of slices of spit-roasted pork in a tortilla with a garnish of onions, coriander and pineapple.

p.16: 'The King' ['El Rey'] is a well-known *ranchera* (a song sung by one person with a guitar during the Mexican Revolution, associated with mariachi groups), composed and most famously sung by José Alfredo Jiménez. The lyrics in Spanish are 'No tengo trono ni reina, ni nadie que me comprenda, pero sigo siendo el rey' [I don't have a throne or a queen, or anyone who understands me, but I'm still the king]. Villalobos has changed the lyrics slightly (from 'anyone who understands me' to 'anyone to keep me'), as this was how he used to sing it as a child.

p.19: *mole* – a thick Mexican chilli sauce combining complex flavours, or a dish based on this sauce. Ingredients can include black pepper, cumin, cloves, aniseed, tomatoes, onion, bread, garlic, sesame seeds, dried fruit and chocolate.

p.19: *tampiqueña* – marinated steak served with cheese and enchiladas or tortilla chips.

p.25: charro – a traditional Mexican horseman, somewhat like the North American cowboy. Charros take part in *charreadas* (a little like rodeos), and wear very distinctive colourful clothing, including a wide-brimmed hat.

p.45: Poza Rica – a medium-sized industrial city in the state of Veracruz. Founded in 1951 and with a skyline dominated by modern buildings and the remnants of the local oil industry, it is not renowned for its beauty.

p.45: La Chona – the local name for the city of Encarnación de Díaz, a town in the state of Jalisco, also not renowned for its beauty.

p. 54: naco – a derogatory Mexican term, quite close to the English slang word 'chav'. It means a vulgar person with no class, style or education, and tends to be used by people from the dominant class to refer to those of the lower class, although it is malleable and can also be used about 'new money'.

p. 59: the Cowboy Mouse (*el ratón vaquero*) was a very evocative 1930s Mexican children's song composed by Francisco Gabilondo Soler, about an English-speaking mouse with a cowboy hat and two pistols.

Dear readers,

With the right book we can all travel far. And yet British publishing is, with illustrious exceptions, often unwilling to risk telling these other stories.

Subscriptions from readers make our books possible. They also help us approach booksellers, because we can demonstrate that our books already have readers and fans. And they give us the security to publish in line with our values, which are collaborative, imaginative and 'shamelessly literary' (Stuart Evers, *Guardian*).

All subscribers to our upcoming titles
- are thanked by name in the books
- receive a numbered, first edition copy of each book (limited to 300 copies for our 2011 titles)
- are warmly invited to contribute to our plans and choice of future books

Subscriptions are:
£20 – 2 books (two books per year)
£35 – 4 books (four books per year)

To find out more about subscribing, and rates for outside Europe, please visit: http://www.andotherstories.org/subscribe/

Thank you!

To find out about upcoming events and reading groups (our foreign-language reading groups help us choose books to publish, for example) you can
- join the mailing list at: www.andotherstories.org
- follow us on twitter: @andothertweets
- join us on Facebook: And Other Stories

This book was made possible by our advance subscribers' support – thank you so much!

Our Subscribers

Aca Szabo
Alexandra Cox
Ali Smith
Alisa Holland
Alison Hughes
Amanda Jones
Amanda Hopkinson
Ana Amália Alves da Silva
Ana María Correa
Anca Fronescu
Andrea Reinacher
Andrew Tobler
Andrew Blackman
Angela Kershaw
Anna Milsom
Anne Christie
Anne Withers
Anne Jackson
Barbara Glen
Bárbara Freitas
Briallen Hopper
Bruce Millar
Carlos Tamm
Carol O'Sullivan
Caroline Rigby
Catherine Mansfield
Cecilia Rossi
Charles Boyle
Charlotte Ryland
Christina MacSweeney
Claire Williams
Clare Horackova
Daniel Hahn
Daniel Gallimore
David Wardrop
Debbie Pinfold
Denis Stillewagt
Elena Cordan

Emma Staniland
Eric Dickens
Eva Tobler-Zumstein
Fiona Quinn
Fiona Miles
Gary Debus
Genevra Richardson
Georgia Panteli
Geraldine Brodie
Hannes Heise
Helen Leichauer
Helen Weir
Henriette Heise
Henrike Lähnemann
Iain Robinson
Ian Goldsack
Jennifer Higgins
Jimmy Lo
Jo Luloff
John Clulow
Jonathan Ruppin
Jonathan Evans
Joy Tobler
Judy Garton-Sprenger
Julia Sanches
Juro Janik
K L Ee
Kate Griffin
Kate Pullinger
Kate Wild
Kevin Brockmeier
Krystalli Glyniadakis
Laura Watkinson
Laura McGloughlin
Liz Tunnicliffe
Lorna Bleach
Louise Rogers
Maisie Fitzpatrick

Margaret Jull Costa
Marion Cole
Nichola Smalley
Nick Stevens
Nick Sidwell
Nicola Hearn
Nicola Harper
Olivia Heal
Peter Law
Peter Blackstock
Philip Leichauer
Polly McLean
Rachel McNicholl
Rebecca Whiteley
Rebecca Miles
Rebecca Carter
Rebecca K. Morrison
Réjane Collard
Ros Schwartz
Ruth Martin
Samantha Schnee
Samantha Christie
Samuel Willcocks
Sophie Moreau
    Langlais
Sophie Leighton
Sorcha McDonagh
Steph Morris
Susana Medina
Tamsin Ballard
Tania Hershman
Tim Warren
Tomoko Yokoshima
Verena Weigert
Vivien Kogut Lessa
    de Sa
Will Buck
Xose de Toro

Our first four titles, published in autumn 2011:

Iosi Havilio, *Open Door*
translated from the Spanish by Beth Fowler

Deborah Levy, *Swimming Home*

Clemens Meyer, *All the Lights*
translated from the German by Katy Derbyshire

Juan Pablo Villalobos, *Down the Rabbit Hole*
translated from the Spanish by Rosalind Harvey

Title: *Down the Rabbit Hole*
Author: Juan Pablo Villalobos
Translator: Rosalind Harvey
Editors: Sophie Lewis, Zaibun Pasha
Proofreader: Wendy Toole
Typesetter: Charles Boyle
Series and Cover Design: Joseph Harries
Format: 210 x 138 mm
Paper: Munken Premium White 80gsm FSC
Printer: T. J. International Ltd, Padstow, Cornwall

The first 300 copies are individually numbered.